Old Knucklebone

P. J. Atwater

This is a work of fiction. Names, characters, places, and incidents are products of the author's imagination or are used fictitiously and are not to be construed as real. Any resemblance to actual events, locations, organizations, or persons, living or dead, is entirely coincidental.

World Castle Publishing, LLC
Pensacola, Florida

Paperback ISBN: 9798891262201
eBook ISBN: 9798891262218
First Edition World Castle Publishing, LLC, July 23, 2024
http://www.worldcastlepublishing.com

Licensing Notes

Cover: Jenna Augustine Atwater
Editor: Karen Fuller

CHAPTER 1

Wintry night had settled over the inn. Through the great hall's squat window, stars shone – some clear, some rimed in frosty halos, winking through black-velvet wisps of floating cloud. The window was of rare glass, and its latticed pane was flecked with a sparse melt of snowflakes: tiny, irresolute pioneers who perished upon contact with the hall's meager glow. A hearth dominated the main floor, and logs crackled dutifully in the widow Mladena's stove in back, bringing the smell of savory cakes and lamb from the kitchen; yet even with the hearth and a myriad of lamps and candles, the hall seemed dim tonight, the rafters low, the freeze a mere breath away, so that the three gamblers at one table sat hunched with their elbows around their drinks and their cloaks on their backs. They spoke in murmurs, as though fearful that drowning out the snap of the hearth would too douse its warmth, and when the door opened on the whistling night, they bunched themselves tighter into their cloaks.

Grimka, the old hunter, squealed a chair to an empty space at the table, eliciting a wince from the others. The widow, knowing what he liked, brought hot wine with his lamb and placed it before him. He thanked her, and he blessed her. She went back to her kitchen, knowing she'd be paid before he was done.

Grimka breathed heavily, rubbing

his doeskin gloves against his elbows. You might be fooled into thinking you could still see his breath in the fire's hazy glow. Brushing slush from his hard, furred shoulders, he looked to his fellows.

"By Knarus, aren't there any logs on the fire?" he said. "Ton, won't you move your chair and let an old man put his back to the hearth a minute?"

Ton grunted and scooted his seat over.

With a grateful mutter, the hunter shifted into the space. The fire dried the sleet but did not reach his frame through his wolfskin cloak. He took off his gloves and pulled his plate close. The meat scalded his fingertips and palate but warmed his belly. He took it all with gratitude. Across the room, his eyes fell upon the totem that hung over the doorframe: a dagger-sized replica of a fat southern sword, pointed down as if poised to thrust on the head of every guest passing through. Crafted from a single piece of iron, it was the emblem of some foreign god brought by a traveler at a time no one remembered. Why Mladena kept it there in place of the traditional Tribefather or her family gods, Grimka did not know and had never asked.

The inn was old and nameless. The family who built it had gone long ago; some said they had perished, though few in the small village would speak openly of such things. The second story sported four private rooms, half of which were occupied by regular boarders: men with no families but with fortune enough to live out their days. Half of the ground floor was occupied by the great hall facing the kitchen; stout wooden walls divided the other half into smaller parlors, which could be filled with cots brought in from the barn. A massive, round stone hearth sat at the intersection of these partitions. It was the very heart of the inn, facing into every room. Each face had copper shutters, so the warmth could be directed into any room at will.

The quaint furnishings, the must of old varnish mingling with Mladena's soaps, and the tinge of cooking and smoke, usually soothed Grimka. He often joked that the widow's house was the only place to keep him, for everything in it was old but fit and well cared for. But tonight, it felt a little less like home.

The dice clunked across the table. They rattled against the wooden side of Mordek's cup. Ton groaned, and Yvorr grinned. Grimka paid no attention. Wiping wine from his beard, setting his cup down, he cast his gaze about the hall.

"But where is Venslas?" He asked.

Ton scooped the dice into his hand.

Draining the last of his wine, he shook a few drops out of his cup and rattled the dice inside—a gesture, the woodcutter claimed, that brought luck when he was down. "He's packing his things," Ton said absently. "Moving on."

Grimka was shocked. "Moving on?"

Ton threw the dice. They came out with a spatter on the stained wood boards. He looked at them and grimaced. "So he says." He passed the dice to Grimka.

"He's lived here ages," said Grimka. He threw the dice, barely noting his roll, and passed them left to Yvorr. "What does he want to leave for?" If Grimka was old, then Mladena's favorite tenant was venerable—too ancient to pull up stakes.

"Venslas says the air here has changed," Yvorr answered. He cast a throw, sucked his teeth in cautious satisfaction, and passed the stones to his left. With a shudder, Grimka pulled the wolfskin tight about his chest. Normally, he'd shed the cloak and coat to let his underclothes dry, but the air had indeed changed, and he felt reluctant to take off any layer. It was as if the pelt were a plate against a sword that might come at any time from behind.

Mordek let the dice sit before his empty bowl, untossed and forgotten. "It's changed, all right," the farmer said. "It changed the night that stranger stayed here. We ought to have done more than just drave him out. Ought to have—"

Ton hissed at him. The table jumped as he kicked him into silence. Mordek left the thought unfinished.

"Nothing good comes of mentioning such things," Yvorr agreed. He called the widow over for another wine.

The men went back to stolidly throwing dice while their hostess made a circuit of the table with her pitcher. Grimka waited until she was gone again—it seemed somehow important to keep women separate from this conversation. From the corner of one eye, he dared to let his gaze linger on her departing form. He noted the shape of her waist under her plain skirts, still good after all these years. The fastidious knot of hair, showing the first signs of gray, settled just above a neck too pale and too long to be covered. She was tall and straight. She carried herself like a countess in her keep.

"Fellows," he said when at last she was out of sight, "I've been on the trail a moon and a half." The dice were pushed toward him, and he slid them along without throwing. "What have I missed out on? You must let me know."

Ton sniffed. Mordek looked questingly to his fellows. It was Yvorr who spoke.

"Not two weeks ago, a foreign man came. Paid a week's lodgings to the widow – up front."

"Foreign? From where?"

"Wouldn't say," Yvorr answered. "But he had a funny way of speech, so he was no Valt."

Mordek interjected. "Riav, and do not doubt!"

The table bounced with another thump, and Mordek winced. "Speak not that name," Ton growled. "We do not know where he was from."

Grimka mused. In his father's day, you could spot a Riav as easy as a parsnip among pears, but the Empire in the East had since conquered many tribes and culled out the unbending. With each generation, their spies became more convincing, pulled from an increasing pool of Western stock. His travels took him to lands where such worries were commonly voiced.

Yvorr went on. "I was here, Venslas at my side, when the man came in. Bartered in ivory for his board. Looked to me like the widow got the better of the bargain, but he didn't seem to mind. His eyes were dark. Almost black."

"Dark like a Riav's"

"Not shaped like Riav eyes," Yvorr said impatiently, annoyed by the interruption but forgetting the breach of taboo. He was in the swing of tale-telling. "But they were uncanny eyes. Unnatural cold – you'd shiver if he looked at you. He looked up and around, like he was listening to the rats in the rafters. Then he says to the widow, plain as if he was telling her there was a faire in a fortnight, 'You have a spirit in your house.'"

Ton's eyes blazed. "Don't blame me," Yvorr told him. "It's what he said. Can't tell the story without it."

The superstitious woodsman grumbled with an air of defeat. He did not bother reminding everyone that he had never been for telling the story.

Mordek seethed. "Wish I'd been there. I'd have fired up the tar on the spot if you'd let me. He all but announced himself a witch."

The others ignored him. "Of course, the widow told him she knew all about the ghost of the inn. 'Don't you mind if you sense something,' she told him. 'Some souls do. It's a friendly spirit, who helps care for the place.'"

"She thinks it's a domovoi," Mordek interjected with a superior air. "Or some kind of kindly elf. Leaves cakes out each night as if she had a brownie." Everyone knew this.

"I know what elf eats those sweets at night," Yvorr put in jocularly. "And she sleeps in the widow's bed."

"Aye. And little Olynka knows the right of it, as do I. It's the ghost of that murdered girl—"

Ton kicked again. This time, the dice and dishes rattled. "Mordek," he said, "must you insist on speaking of the accursed?"

Mordek flinched, looking as if he would answer the rebuke in kind, but Yvorr diffused them both with another jest: "And on taking your wisdom from a girl of eleven years?" He and Ton both snickered. Mordek looked from one to the other but only shook his head. Grimka clutched his cup between his fingers and waited for the tale to continue. He was beginning to feel the warmth of the fire at his back and the meal in his belly, but his skin yet tingled as if in an icy draft.

"He took the room between me and Venslas..." Yvorr began, picking up the yarn again without preamble.

Grimka stopped him. "Eh? The middle room? I thought that was yours, Yvorr."

Yvorr shook his head. "Since harvest, the old man's snoring has gotten worse. The widow let me move my things down the hall."

"Ah. Continue, please."

"Well, we'd all turned in, as usual: me at my end of the hall, old Venslas at his, Mladena and Olynka down by the kitchen, and the outsider there in between Venslas and me. I listened like I normally do for the sounds of our fairy from my bed, but all I heard were the rats before I fell asleep.

"I got woken up late in the night—I guess it was nearly the fourth hour. I heard a man yelling in the room next to me. 'I know you are here! Show yourself, I command you!'"

Unconsciously, Yvorr had raised his voice as he mimicked the stranger's cries. It was the first loud noise to this point, save for the wind. The widow stuck her head out of the kitchen and fixed Yvorr with a dark look. "Olynka is sleeping," was all she said, but her tone and face said more. After a single, slow shake of her graying locks, she left them.

Speaking low, Yvorr went on. "Anyhow, that's the gist of what he was saying. 'Reveal yourself to me, you cannot resist me,' and all the rest." Even Ton was giving his full attention now. The dice had been clutched in Mordek's sweaty white hand for many minutes. "Still half-asleep as I was, I'd forgotten about changing rooms. I thought there must be someone breaking into Venslas' apartment. I went where I heard the voices, and I threw myself against the door – almost broke it right down. I'd had only two goes at it with my shoulder before the widow was at my back with her old crossbow. I even saw old Venslas poke himself into the corridor – so at least I might have known he was safe – but I still had one foot in my dream and the rest of me was blind with fury. Before I could make sense out of anything I had the door open.

"There was that damnable outlander, standing in the middle of the apartment floor, hands on his sides, still dressed in his travel clothes, glaring at us like we'd just interrupted his morning squat n' shave. Glaring with those black eyes that made you feel icy when they looked at you. He was indignant and demanded that we leave him, the mad rascal. But the widow and I paid no mind. It didn't take long for the two of us to piece together what he'd been about. Olynka I think was watching it all from the stair. What all he was doing in there – he had candles lit, and… through the door, we'd heard him speaking… conversing… and I swear he was answered by… well, maybe Ton wouldn't appreciate my telling the details." He shifted in his chair. Ton studied his thumbs on the table. "Well, it wasn't long until daylight anyway, so the widow and I decided we'd watch him until the sun came up and then decide what to do with him. She wanted to hand me the bow but I told her to keep it since it doesn't take any strength to pull a trigger. I took my mace from under my bed while she held the crossbow on him, and we stayed like that, all three of us standing until the end of the night. Then she sent Olynka out to gather all the men from around. Mordek and Ton here answered the call, and many others.

We had a short meeting right there in the hall, and we decided to tell the stranger he had till noon to get out of sight and stay, or we'd run him up a tree. Before he left, he laughed – I'm sure he was mad – and he lays a curse on all of us: 'There will be murder in your village. Murder, before the first storm's end in winter.'"

Ton nodded grimly as if confirming the whole story – and not just the parts he'd seen. Mordek slapped the tabletop, and the dice scattered from his fist.

"Tar and feather would have served him better," he spat.

"You just want to tar and feather somebody," Ton said soberly.

"Not just anybody," Mordek argued. "But a Riav, necromancing son of…"

"So, after this…" Grimka interrupted.

All at once, the three fell silent.

Yvorr gazed into his cup. The hearth seemed to suddenly dim – or perhaps it had died slowly, and the men had only noticed now.

"Olynka's having bad dreams," Yvorr said slowly. "She doesn't say much, as you know, but I wake and hear her many nights. Her mother thinks she took a fright, seeing the… what we saw in that room. Only… only old Ven's having them, too. And not just when he's awake, he…"

All four men jumped at a sudden thump overhead. A drift of dust scattered from the crossbeam to sprinkle the table.

"A rat," Mordek said.

The hunter bent his keen ears rafterward. "No rat," he said. Ton shot a glare around the table, one that said, *I warned the lot of you.*

"*Shhh,*" said Yvorr, though no one was speaking. There proceeded a series of heavy thump-creaks, like heavy boots traversing the upper floor.

"It's the old man, then," Mordek said. He was suddenly hushed and wan.

"I've never heard Venslas move that way," said Grimka. "And besides, it must be nigh on midnight."

"Like I said, he's fed up," said Yvorr. "Probably hauling a full trunk across the room. He swears he'll leave tomorrow."

"I expect he'll be up all night preparing his things." Ton appeared grateful, almost cheerful, to have found a natural explanation.

The men leaned back, humming at the satisfactory explanation, though Grimka remained misgiven. The thumping had stopped, and it passed eagerly out of memory. Mordek was looking out the window. "Blast, it *is* almost midnight." He hurried out of his chair, tightening the fastens on his cloak reflexively. "I'll freeze my chin off riding home."

"We've stayed too late," Grimka told him. "Share a bed with me; I'll put you up. The wife will understand."

"Hell, she will," said Mordek, getting his hat. "It's me sharing beds that concerns her."

Ton drained his cup in a quaff. "Well, mine will tan me, but she'll just have to tan me. You couldn't get me out in that cold."

"And you couldn't get me to lay down in this place, not for a wink. Not anymore. Good night, friends." Mordek shivered, perhaps anticipating the frost, and turned for the door. "The snow's stopped, at least."

Suddenly, Yvorr rose too. "Slow down, Mordek. You shouldn't walk alone; I'll go with you."

"Thanks, Yvorr, but I've got a horse and a good lamp. I'll be home before you miss me."

"Come back for dinner, so we'll know you've been safe."

"Sure, Grimka. Good night."

They watched him go, and each man was on his feet in that communal instinct that informs a group of friends when the night has ended. Ton put a log in the hearth. As he turned away, the dying flame took it slowly. "If you're still offering to split a bed, Grimka," he said, "I'd be much obliged." Grimka nodded.

"I'm off to bed, then," said Yvorr. "After I leak." He headed for the side door.

"I could go, too," said Ton, going after him.

"I'll get the key from Mladena," Grimka said. "Which room do you like, Ton? The middle one has the widest bed." He chuckled at the woodcutter's humorless look. "See you upstairs, Ton."

The kitchen was dark except for a dull, rusty hue from a low fire. Leaning in through the door, he saw both women in their bed beside the stove. Olynka had curled herself around her mother's feet, where her back was nearest the heat. Their black mousehunter was tucked into a niche between their bodies. The cat tilted its head and watched him with half an open green eye, ears flat. Grimka reached around the doorframe and slid his hand up the wall until he felt the key hooks, hoping he had found the right one in the dark. As the key tinkled in his grasp, the widow shifted onto her back, showing the long white of her neck beneath her nightdress. Grimka tried not to dwell on the vague longing excited within him by that helpless beauty; he thought he might reach down to the furs and cover her again but decided against even that. There was a small shelf beneath the keys. Grimka reached into the folds of his many clothes and pulled out some coins. Counting the money in the dark proved difficult, and he was sure he left more than he owed, but he remembered all the times the widow had undercharged him. "Bless you, girls," he breathed. Then he touched his brow in salute to the cat and said, "You too, fellow huntsman."

The cat kept one eye through the doorway as the old man in his wolf pelt snuffed the candles and turned the wicks on the lamps. Long after he was gone, the cat still watched. At length, he opened his other eye too — he opened them wide. His ears pointed up, and he became rigid, peering into the deepening shadows that stretched forth from the dying hearth. The girl groaned and fretted, shifting with knitted brows. Without waking, the widow cooed to her. The black cat stood and sprang away.

CHAPTER 2

Grimka stirred from a fitful sleep filled with vague and confused dreams. He woke at the same time every day, as the first light touched the eastern sky, but a glance at the black, frosted window told him that hour was long off. Ton snored on his back with one arm spread across Grimka's chest and the other dangling over the edge of the narrow bed. Grimka's bladder was bothering him. Not for the first time, he wondered when, at his age, he would learn to decline the second round of Mladena's wine.

Grimka got his cloak from where it

hung by the door and wrapped himself in it. Then he went for his boots. He was used to the cold, but while sitting on his father's knee, he'd heard of a eunuch whose castration had resulted from his piss freezing up inside him while he went: had he just had shoes in the cold, his manhood would be safe. It was a tale too preposterous, but it had left a deep impression on the boy that the old man could not shake.

He was midway through lacing up his second boot when he heard a creak in the corridor. Then another.

Even in his thick boots, Grimka could creep up on a deer in the woods close enough to count the burrs in its antlers. With such stealth did he crack the door and peer along the passage. At the far end, away from the stair, was a large window, the foggy, moon-silvered pane given scant cover by a pair of threadbare curtains. The corridor was as still as a held breath; not so much as a draft invaded to rustle the window drapes, and even the rats were asleep. Yet the huntsman's instincts were afire, warning him of a lurking menace.

Once, many years ago, Grimka had been stalked by a wolf pack in the forest. He'd been careless and was lucky to have escaped with his life. He rarely told the tale, for there was nothing to boast of; for whatever reason, the beasts ultimately decided against attacking him and went off to chase other prey. The most frightful part of the ordeal had been when their howls had gone silent, for he knew they were encircling him then, pacing his movements with patience, concealed among the trees. He could feel them ringing him with unseen, menacing eyes. He had this same feeling as he went through the dark house. The coals in the hearth gave less light than the starlight at the windows, and none of it reached the stairwell. He went with a practiced stealth. He knew the stairs in Mladena's inn like he knew the terrain of the forest, and navigating by touch and memory, he stepped carefully around the spots he knew would creak. He did his business as quickly and as quietly as he could.

On his way back up, he paused. A subtle change in the silver light suffusing the top of the stair might have been a cloud crossing the moon, but his senses told him it was something much closer. Was that a creak in the hall? It sounded like the fourth floorboard from the far window—the one before Venslas' door. He wished he had thought to carry his knife; he longed for a weapon. He was near paralyzed, dreading the top hallway as much as the drafty darkness below. Yet he could not sleep on the stair. The stair turned a corner just before the last few steps, affording cover from which one could peek. He tiptoed upward and slowly inched an eye across the upper landing.

He saw a hulking man standing with shoulders squared before the far window. He was standing straight but with his head lowered. With the only poor light shining behind the form, Grimka could not tell if he was facing the stair or the window. For an instant, he thought it might be Yvorr, for he seemed to be holding a long-shafted weapon in his hands like the mace his old friend kept under his bed. But this man was far larger than Yvorr.

Grimka did not know how long he stood there, his hand on the corner post, his old heart palpitating, his eye fixed on that terrifying form. He was frozen in earnest now. He had never been more afraid in his life. He'd have gladly traded places with his younger self, surrounded by wolves in the cold night.

At length, the man raised his head as if harkening to something. Grimka nearly fainted — had he been noticed? But no, old Venslas had hitched into a robust bout of his infamous snoring. The man in the hall turned, and with a new, unaccountable chill, Grimka realized he had been facing the window. He reached for Venslas' door, hefting the weapon — Grimka saw the fat blade of a wood axe, black against the moonlight — opened it, and stepped heavily inside. The door closed behind him with a click.

Sprinting on silent tiptoes, avoiding by instinct the noisier boards, Grimka flew to his bedchamber. "Ton," he whispered harshly, shaking the grunting woodsman awake. "Awake, Ton. Someone is in the house. I think he means to harm old Venslas."

Ton's eyes were open at these words. "What? A man? What man? Are you sure?"

"I don't know," Grimka answered all the questions at once. "Come." Slipping his long knife from the belt hanging on the bedpost, he said, "Have you something to fight with?"

Ton grabbed a small hatchet from the windowsill by the bed. In an instant, he was in the hall in his bare feet and underclothes. "Go get Yvorr," he ordered, and he rushed noisily to Venslas' door.

It seemed to take an agonizingly long time rousing Yvorr and drawing him from bed. He had taken more wine than anyone; he slept heavily and woke groggily. But by the time he was back in the hall, Yvorr and his long mace by his side, Grimka realized he had heard no other sounds in the meantime, only the continued snoring of the old man.

Venslas' door hung open. Ton came out to meet them, the hatchet hanging in his grasp. "I don't know what you saw, Grimka, but the old man's unharmed." He paused, giving a chance for the others to hear the snores. "You say you saw a man? Are you sure?"

Grimka ignored the questioning. "Did you open the cupboards? The closets, the wardrobe, all?"

Ton nodded. "Of course I did. He's alone, and safe. He didn't even wake."

"What did you get me out of bed for, Grimka?" Yvorr grumbled. He lifted his nightshirt to scratch his belly. He still had his nightcap on.

"I'll have a look myself," Grimka began. He stopped. There was a creak on the stair.

"What is all this?" The widow called from the darkness. "Who's up here charging about?" Grimka didn't need to see her to know the old crossbow was leveled in their general direction. He noted with some measure of satisfaction, almost purely professional in nature, that his hiding spot around the corner had been almost totally obscured by shadow. The widow emerged from it now, the weapon poised.

"Grimka thinks he saw our ghost," Yvorr said.

Grimka was startled by the blunt, almost flippant mention of the supernatural. "I did, ma'am." He said. He started to explain what he'd seen.

The widow shook her head. "I don't know what you saw, but we can speak of it over breakfast. Please. No talk of ghosts at this hour."

"Yes, ma'am." Grimka nodded. Ton held his peace and dragged his feet toward their bed. Yvorr paused long enough to say something sarcastic that Grimka didn't really hear. The widow bade them all good night and no more jumping on the floorboards or shouting until dawn. Grimka sensed her pause in the darkness of the stairwell.

"My sweetcake, I told you to stay below. Get back into bed," he heard her say. There were two sets of footsteps going down the stairs after that—one much lighter and more reticent than the other.

Grimka was the last into bed. Though weary to his bones, he spent a long time listening to Ton's heavy breathing before slumber took him, and his dreams were all the more troubled.

CHAPTER 3

They did not, in fact, speak more of the ghost in the morning. Grimka burned to have it addressed, but the others comported themselves with an air of solemnity and introspection. At this breakfast table, there was suddenly no appetite for ghosts, so meekly Grimka let it rest.

Meals in the inn included fowl from Grimka's own hunt, and he spent much of the next couple of days bringing the last of his latest pelts into market. He always brought a portion of his finest kills to the widow. Despite having sent two wives and three sons to the pyre, he felt life had been kind enough to him. She repaid him by roasting his catches lovingly and putting them on his plate with plenty of gravy and wild rosemary. The smokehouse in back worked night and day.

Ton spent little time in the inn, stopping by only for a beer with dinner and leaving before dark. Mordek and others came and went, but it was largely just Grimka and Yvorr staying there with the women.

Olynka's moods were alternately dark and bright. Her only joys were found in the yard, playing alone or with the neighbor's boy, where the sunlight seemed to burn away the malaise that accompanied her indoor chores. At the end of chores, her mother would send her out with her favorite treat: a fresh-peeled purple carrot. Grimka flinched unaccountably as she snapped the tip like a rabbit between bucky front teeth. He shivered, and his fingers tingled. This was one of her few indulgences; at dinner, she would poke at her coldening meals, one time complaining she had difficulty swallowing anything. Indeed, she would choke and gag when trying to take food. She even coughed when biting her carrots. The widow peered down her mouth and declared her free of laryngitis. Nonetheless, she took on a piqued, sickly look, especially within the shadow of the house. Indoors, she hunched about, wary as harried game, yet beyond vague complaints, she seemed unable to voice what troubled her.

Venslas, despite his talk the first night of hurrying on, was delayed. "It's unbearable here," the ancient would say with a curse, "but I am too old to be moving on. Where would I stay that was any better? I'm just too tired to move." His packed trunks sat in odd places around the room while he stayed in his bed most of the day, snoring for long hours. At intervals when he fell silent, Grimka or Yvorr or the widow would go upstairs to check on him, to find him alive but still sleeping. He would let out a sudden snort, roll over, and go back to snoring.

He was ailing, the widow declared, and the narrow down mattress was like to become his deathbed. Grimka thought it a grave tragedy that he should have his deathbed in a house he no longer liked because he was plagued by ghosts—and Grimka *did* believe in the ghosts—but he left this unsaid.

Grimka saw the widow's daughter, gaunt and hollow eyed from sleeplessness and fear. His youngest boy would be not much older than Olynka was now, and he often thought how none of his sons had married. He'd have liked to have a daughter like her, and he supposed the girls *had* become family to him, in a sense. When he thought of anything happening to them... they needed this inn, like he needed his spears.

The girl was outside, catching bugs with the boy her age who lived across the field. The days had faired up after that slushy night they had not spoken of, and the sun was warm and bright, though the wind still carried the tundric chill off the distant steppe. Grimka stood at the stoop, watching them across the terrace. He leaned on the broom he had just used to sweep the dried mud—a favor to his landlady—looking like a sleepy sentinel with his halberd. The widow came out with two steaming cups of mulled juice.

"A bit old for chasing dragonflies," Grimka remarked, watching the flecks of clove move as he swirled his cup.

The widow nodded. "A bit young to go sleepless with care."

Grimka studied her as she said this. She looked sleepless herself, though he supposed he'd always be taken with her beauty. He'd known her before her husband. It had taken years to get used to the idea she was his; now, he could easily forget he was gone. The former innkeeper had passed through the fire, as all men must—he'd be waiting for his wife, Grimka reminded himself with a pang of loneliness.

"You disbelieve the…" Grimka paused, guarding his words, for he found himself dreading the mention of certain things of late, the same as Ton. "... the *presence* in the inn."

Her slim shoulders shrugged, barely, a mere shifting of her shawl. "I have always known there was a presence.

Now, the sweets I leave go untouched; the little chores we'd find done overnight are left undone, and we have no protection against evil dreams. The dark easterner drove our domovoi out with his curses—what else could explain it?"

An evil dream? Is that what I saw in the hall? Grimka thought with a touch of frustration. There was much that went against the friendly elf theory.

The widow's gaze was out across the corral to the barn. She drained her cup. "Speaking of chores undone," she said, as if to herself. Then she called, "Sweetcake, tell your friend to run home. The butter is warm; time to bake bread!"

Grimka saw the laughter melt away from the girl's eyes as they turned toward the house, replaced by that hollow grimness that had become their feature. Yet she obeyed her mother, and while her playmate scampered over the field, she trudged toward the kitchen.

With a brief touch to Grimka's arm, the widow turned to the door, walking before her daughter. She stumbled at the threshold with a tiny cry, for something laying underfoot tripped her up.

It was the sword-shaped charm that had hung over the entrance. With a cluck, the woman adjusted her skirts and stooped to pick it up. "How strange," she remarked to Grimka, dusting the false edge with her fingertips; "That has never fallen from its place before."

She stretched herself out on her toes toward a pair of hooked, ginger-colored nails planted over the doorframe to support the hilt. Seeing her struggle, Grimka stepped in gently to lend his height. The charm was heavy in his calloused hands. Unconsciously, he ran his fingers over it as she had and found it dented on one side, the blunt blade flattened as if in impact. His brow creased, and he studied the damage, troubled by thoughts he would not have voiced aloud, for it would have done no good. The widow and her daughter watched him, the latter tensely and the former with an air of impatience; it was as if they could not proceed until they saw the sword was secure.

At last, he satisfied them by hanging it back on its nails. A fleck of rust broke off one of the nails and fluttered out the door on an unfelt breeze. No rust marred the surface of the charm itself. The widow turned her back promptly, urging Olynka toward the kitchen. The girl kept the icon in the corner of her eye the whole way.

Grimka, too, was unwilling to keep his back fully to the door and the sword as he lit slowly for the stair and his quarters. He would lie back on his bed and ponder for a while, for he was deeply misgiven. Surely, the iron figure had fallen sometime while he and the widow were on the trellis, or else it would have tripped her on her way out to stand by him…

He paused by a shelf near the stair, where a stout brazen bowl lay empty. With a tremulous hand, he grasped it. By his senses, its weight was similar to that of the iron charm. Near enough. After long consideration, he held out his hand and dropped the bowl to the floor.

Thud. The sound of brass striking the hollow floor was audible throughout the chamber.

A queasy feeling lurched over in Grimka's insides, his dreaded hypothesis confirmed. Why had neither he nor the widow heard the sword fall?

***

The sun was low, and already, the

first lights of the village down the road were becoming visible. The evening's bread filled the yard with its redolence, the barn was clean, and the clothesline flapped with an array of woolen banners. A new wind had striped the sky over the village with a pink and orange cloudy patina. It was already becoming cold.

Grimka came around the house with an armload of fresh-split firewood, Yvorr close behind in kind. The hunter was thinking of the coins he had brought in after his last hunt. The trail had been kind to him with a bounty in meat and pelts, yet the wages would run out before winter's end. The season was yet young, and there might be time for a catch or two before the freeze became unendurable, but could he leave the widow and the child behind? He did not doubt the widow would extend credit, but he disliked the idea of asking. He wanted only what he could be sure to pay for. So, knowing Yvorr took on the odd chore to mitigate his own expenses, he had offered to help. There ought to be plenty of men's work to go around.

Olynka's playmate had returned after the afternoon chores. The two had found a couple of long, straight branches and were playing at knights and squires while their twin shadows stretched and paled across the inn's wood facade. They were in the midst of a debate over who ought to be knight and who the squire when abruptly Yvorr set his pile down and tapped Grimka's shoulder.

"I say, someone is about to arrive for dinner."

Holding his burden to him, Grimka strained his eyes to the road. A horseman had come over a hill, still too distant for the trotting to be heard.

"Do you think it's Mordek?" Yvorr

asked.

"He's about the only soul who comes up here anymore," Grimka answered. As he watched, two more horsemen followed. The orange sun glinted off their steel-clad shoulders. An unaccountable thrill raced through Grimka's heart at the sight. It was rare to see warriors riding through.

"Men-at-arms always make me think of trouble," Yvorr grumbled.

Grimka shook his head. "Likely some lord traveling alone. Enough of them these days. They need beds just the same as small folk."

"Hope this one likes ghosts."

The two kept quiet and watched the horses, Grimka only resting his woodpile after a moment. When the riders had come quite near, the children took notice. They rushed down the road to see. Yvorr started after them nervously, but Grimka slowed him with a hand, for he could see the man in front indeed was Mordek, his Mien cheerful. By the time they had made their way there, the two youths could be heard chattering at the two armored men.

The warriors were harnessed in gleaming links of steel astride massive, doughty warmounts. Burnished sallets hung clanking from the saddle bags, along with pieces of plate armor bundled in cloth. In one motion, the taller one swung from the saddle to greet the children, graceful even on stiff limbs and road-sore spine. He was black-haired with a beard as thick as woven silk. The ice-blue of his intelligent eyes sparkled mirthfully as he indulged the children's questions. His shoulders were back and his spine straight, a posture of grace born of strength—one Grimka knew from experience was difficult to maintain after a long ride, which the dust on his boots betrayed. The other was a hand shorter and a few stones lighter, though still massive compared to most men. He remained mounted, looking down with a superior air—though Grimka had an instinctive sense that his was the lower station. His hair was a sandier shade, his beard and moustaches trimmed and fashioned into points, his eyes dark and needle-like. His face held little of the warmth of his larger fellow's. While the taller, black-maned warrior showed grace, if not outright joy, in response to the children, the other appeared determined to endure as long as necessary.

Though clearly fit men, their faces also had the drawn and beleaguered cast Grimka recognized as coming through prolonged travail and hardship. It was the look he had seen on the faces of wolves at the end of winter.

Mordek waved a greeting as they approached. He began to speak, but Olynka broke away and rushed to Grimka and Yvorr, her face alight like they hadn't seen in ages.

"Grimka, Yvorr! Sir Kasmir is a real knight! He's slain goblins and devils and bears and trolls. His squire's brave, too. They're coming to slay the bad ghost."

Grimka looked from the girl to Mordek to the two strangers. Sir Kasmir, he of the black mane, had hardened his expression. He did not nod or shake his head, but he met Grimka's gaze levelly and unreadably. He gave firm, businessly shakes of Grimka and Yvorr's hands in turn. At his back, the squire smirked.

"Sir Kasmir of Tole, Knight Emissary of the True Valtan Order. My squire is Dieter." They exchanged introductions.

Yvorr gave a sardonic smile. "'True

Valta,' eh? You royalists are a long way from home."

"I pass through many a town and camp in hunting season," Grimka put in conversationally. "Your king is the subject of many a debate in the tribal lands."

"Oh? Would I be too forward if I asked what way these debates go?"

Grimka smiled. "You might be, but I'll answer. They go as you might expect: most are against. They are sworn to uphold the rights of the chiefs. There is the common slogan: 'No Kings in Valta, Only Free Men.' The remainder tend toward indifference, and are shouted down and hotly mocked."

"Such a thoughtful motto," Dieter sneered. "Once the Riavs have their way, there will be neither kings *nor* free men!"

"Would you also forgive me asking which side you come down on?"

Grimka shrugged. "Put me in the remainder, I guess."

"Sounds about right. My mission is to change these debates. Might I say, you see us as foreigners, and our ways heterodox and strange. But our tongues and our gods are the same, so we ought at least to be brothers. We have enemies East, West, and South, and the Riavs have spread their conquest far into the free lands of our neighbors. The ancient tribes were united long ago, and I believe in the coming age, unity will mean the difference between survival and eradication."

"Well, sire," said Yvorr with that same sardonic tone, "pray do not ask me what side I lie on. But, as you are peaceable royalists, come up the path with us."

From his saddle, the squire Dieter crowed: "Sir Kasmir, the tribals don't want us, as I told you. Let us take our gold into the forest."

"Dieter, quiet!" the knight commanded with soft force.

But Yvorr told them, "Nay, gentlemen, it's not my house to turn you out of; I only live there. Let the good widow have her say on where your gold shall stay."

The children had stood by, scarcely patient, and had endured as much of the adult pleasantry and politicking as they could. "Sir Kasmir, Sir Kasmir," the neighbor boy yipped, jumping excitedly. The knight's face softened the instant he gave the boy his attention. "What's the worst beast you ever killed?"

All presence of warmth fled the knight's eyes. The smile remained at the lips, but the laughter in the eyes was gone. He gazed a moment as though he could see a long way through the boy.

"Son," he said at last, "I could not speak of that monster, for it is too terrible." He said this with an effort to maintain his joking tone, but the anguish in his voice and eyes was plain to Grimka, and he knew exactly what kind of beast Kasmir was thinking of.

The children took no note; Olynka was already leaping to a new subject. "Nels and I were just playing knights," she said. Grimka caught the squire scoffing under his breath. "He says I can't be a knight. He says I have to be the squire."

"You can't be a knight. You're a girl." Nels declared.

"Well, a farm boy can't be a knight either! Sir, tell him he's wrong!"

Kasmir allowed himself a wry smirk. "What do you say, Dieter?" He turned a cocked eye on the surly squire, who seemed on the brink of dying of boredom. Kasmir seemed to take some playful pleasure in the squire's expression; it was then Grimka thought he caught a faint family resemblance.

"What?" the squire Dieter growled. "Like squiring's so easy? You don't do half the work I do."

Kasmir gave a bark of approving laughter. He turned back to the girl, smiling in truth.

"Listen, sweet girl. How do you suppose I became a knight?"

"I suppose it's because your daddy is a lord." Olynka was sullen, apparently wondering if she was to be humiliated.

"That's a good guess. You're quite smart." Olynka allowed herself to beam cautiously. "That is often the case with knights," he went on, "but not always, not where I'm from. My father was a common sentry. Would you believe it? Dieter's, too—our daddies sat watch on a wall all their lives. I became a knight because I acted the way a knight must."

Grimka decided he had made up his mind, at least about Sir Kasmir; you could judge a hard man by the way he treated children. He would continue to have his eye on the squire.

Mordek took the ensuing silence as an opportunity to interject. "Our guests have already mentioned they are hungry. They've been through sieges and trekked through lean leagues. Away now, children, and let them inside. A body can't hunt ghosts if he's starved to death in his saddle with little urchins chewing his ears off!"

The wind was steadily increasing, and with it, the chill. Thickening clouds hastened the advent of night. Grimka knelt before the boy. "Nels, do you like wolf's teeth?"

The boy nodded rapidly.

"I've got a whole box of them in my room. Good ones. If you help me take the horses to the barn and run along home, then you can have your pick tomorrow."

The child beamed and puffed with the pride of an important job. Rising, Grimka caught Sir Kasmir favoring him with a subtle, kindred smile. Perhaps the knight was making up his own mind about him.

Chapter 4

When Grimka came at last from the stables, all the men were seated at the table near the round, central hearth with drinks before them. Two light riding-hauberks lay folded side-by-side on the bench under the hanging cloaks and hats, and the two warriors sat in fresh, comfortable clothing of courtly quality. The night was settling; it began to feel much like that first night after Grimka's return from the trail. With the women in the kitchen preparing the meal, Mordek was speaking in a hush:

"... ought not to have that child

anywhere near this place, I told her, but get her elsewhere. It's simply unconscionable. I even reminded her of the girl's father – why *he* would never have..."

As Grimka doffed his jacket and boots, from behind the wall there came a succession of violent bumps and squeals. Every soul in the chamber turned to take notice.

Near Grimka's feet, a piece of loose molding shifted aside from the wall, and the widow's black cat came shooting from a hollow space behind with a small rat wriggling feebly in his jaws. Instinctively, Grimka recoiled from the dart-like motion at his feet. Pausing only to censure him with a single, baleful look, the cat darted through the room with the now-dead rat, ahead of anyone trying to challenge his right to the feast. A half a moment later, Mladena could be heard shooing him from the kitchen with an oath. There came another clatter and a clap of wood somewhere in back of the house, and the ratcatcher was gone.

Grimka took the seat that had been set aside for him. Mordek and Yvorr turned to face the center, shaking their heads in jocular chagrin at their own misplaced nerves. The squire Dieter merely sneered at the whole scene, but the intelligent, icy eyes of Sir Kasmir lingered intensely on the spot where the cat had emerged. They traced an invisible pathway along the wall, to the rafters above and across the room. They fixed themselves once upon the metallic icon above the doorframe and then returned to the men about the table, who already were back in the midst of furious yarn-weaving.

It was a queer occurrence with what readiness, what suddenness, the tale came forth after days of abject demur. Perhaps it was the presence of this stranger in shining steel or simply the return of the talkative Mordek that energized the gossip's table all at once. Indeed, Mordek did most of the telling, which contented Grimka, who volunteered only the most recent events to which Mordek was not party; Yvorr stepped in only when one or the other omitted or misrecalled some point he found important. Kasmir patiently parsed through the story, bearing for the most part with the bits that rambled and asking for certain details to be repeated or clarified. His blue eyes scanned the room rhythmically as he listened, as though behind them, a scribe's pen scrawled every word as it was spoken. Dieter, for his part, appeared neither bored nor off-put but attended the story with every interest; it was evident that to him, no less than to his master, the unseemly account was in every way creditable.

"Tell me about the scimitar hung above the door," Kasmir said, leaning back.

As one, the three locals turned in their seats to regard it, as though to confirm it was still there. They shrugged.

"It's been here as long as the widow has," Mordek said. "Her husband, rest him, must have put it there."

"Was he a southman?"

"Sir? Not as far as I can tell."

"I've always wondered about the thing," Yvorr said. "It's just a part of this place, as far as I'm concerned, though I do wonder where it came from."

Kasmir said: "It is a symbol of an old god of the south named Dek. When the Deneirs conquered their empire, his worship was outlawed—but a few of the tribes still pray to him, mostly in secret.

His symbol is used as a ward against spirits—though I suspect you have a forgery, made by no true priest of Dek."

Grimka stiffened at this. He leaned over the table, eager to hear more—just then, the widow and her daughter bustled out under armloads of steaming plates. Brusquely, she presented the men with the day's bread and bowls of stew from Grimka's hunt.

"I am sure our prestigious guests have urgent business," the widow said, as if to the entire table, "and will not wish to stay long."

Sir Kasmir paused, slowly stirring his soup. He studied her carefully. "Madam, have my squire and I given some kind of offense?" The girl looked on, sheepish, behind her mother's skirts.

"Sir knight, your squire and you have been model guests—*so far*—and I am sure you are most welcome to the hospitality of this house. Yet since your arrival, my daughter has done nothing but speak of your great designs."

"Madam, I assure you I have no designs on your house."

"At any rate," said she abruptly, "we can afford no exorcist."

While Kasmir withheld himself, the squire spoke out, "Woman, is charity so far beyond considering?" The look from Kasmir told Grimka he thought this was the wrong move.

"So it's true," the widow said. "Now, listen. Whatever trouble we have began with a foreign troublemaker conjuring spirits for his own peevish delight, and I'll suffer no more of that while I run this house. I'll ask you to keep your well-meaning curiosity to yourselves while you're here, and pray let us keep you no longer than necessary."

With that, she left them in a long

silence. The cold of the night crept in, and the shadows from the edges of the windows seemed to encroach on the edges of the firelight. After the meal, Kasmir bargained for their lodgings and won a night's stay, with a solemn vow that they would do nothing during their stay to disturb the dead.

"You cannot listen to her," Mordek implored in the quiet of after dark. He was standing at the door with the shadows across his face and his cloak draped from his fingers. "She denies what is in front of her—it isn't healthy—and think of the child—"

Kasmir shook his head, slowly. "Though we may agree, I will not act against the mistress of the house."

Mordek bade them all good night and departed, vowing this was not yet settled. Yvorr went to bring a bowl to old Venslas and then turned in for bed.

Kasmir and Dieter turned to retire as well, but Grimka stopped the knight with a hand to his shoulder.

"You must tell me one thing," he pleaded. When Kasmir nodded, he went on. "You had started to say before that the sword icon is not legitimate. What did you mean by that?"

Kasmir glanced at the image. With a look over his shoulder to the quiet kitchen, he strode over to the entryway, easily reaching the holy symbol and taking it down.

"Dek is a god of iron," he explained, running his finger along the same dent Grimka and Mladena had both felt along the edge. "His priests are all smiths, and his icons are always made of iron. Iron has certain properties, they say, that are abominable to spirits."

As he placed the symbol back on its hooks, Grimka's eyes went wide. The hooks were rusted; there was no rust on the sword.

"The first time I saw that dent on the side, I knew it was no charm of pure iron," Kasmir said. "That symbol is made of lead."

CHAPTER 5

Grimka lay on his back and listened to the shrill drone of the feeble wind. He watched the slow, subtle ebb and tide of silver light on the rafters as piebald thunderheads moved across the starry sky. In the moments of darkness, the air above his head seemed to swirl with dancing pockets of inky jet; then the clouds would move, and all was limned in a dull bluish glow.

Voices drew his attention out in the hall. And although he'd relieved himself before coming up, his old bladder was beginning to bother him. He felt a queer thrill as he wrapped himself in his fur cloak and slipped on his soft boots: the hunter on a midnight prowl.

The new guests had taken the "haunted" room in the middle of the hall. A thin waver of candlelight and a thin murmur of voices simmered through the crack at the threshold. There was no reason, which Grimka could examine in the boyish thrill of the deep midnight, for going as he did to press his ear against their door. Venslas' snoring at the end of the hall gave cover to his stealthy tread.

"... may yet change her mind," Kasmir was saying. "It is difficult confronting such business – for some more than others."

"That's all well and good, but what affair is it of ours?"

"Winning the hearts and minds of lords is not all we are charged to do, Dieter. Championing the commons can make our rule easier… or even put pressure on the lords in our favor."

Dieter sniffed audibly. "You've read too deeply into the children's tales. Heroes tromping the globe and righting wrongs for all the little folk."

"There may be something more to those tales than you have understood, cousin."

Before he was done pondering this exchange, Grimka heard a muffled noise and knew Olynka was out of her bed. New curiosity brought him flashing silently to the stair.

His keen eyes were already acclimated to the dark, but the clouds were out, and the shadows were deep in the great hall below. The girl's soft whisper drew his attention to a nook along one of the dividing walls, and just then, the window became effused with brilliant moonlight. He caught sight of the girl's white nightdress, seeming to glow like pearl as it swirled behind her. Her pale arms and even her dark hair seemed vivid with color as she sped on soft tread into one of the smaller parlors and disappeared from sight. He had caught only the briefest glimpse.

She must be chasing the cat, Grimka told himself, but something in the girl's furtive manner had alarmed him. His wildest thoughts flew to Mordek's tale of a girl's ghost, murdered when the inn was new, and slewed back. He took a couple steps down the flight, craning to see through the parlor doorway.

Then he stopped, for someone else stepped into the square of moonlight after her.

She came from the direction of the kitchen, creeping along the same wall on the trail of the little girl. She moved slowly, apprehensively, and Grimka was near enough now to see her features plainly in the silver light. This was Olynka! Who then was she following? Her eyes were wide, and she trembled with each cautious step of her lily-white feet. For some reason, he did not dare call out. She went to the parlor door, glanced once toward the kitchen, where the door was limned in the faintest light of the iron stove, then passed into the next room.

When a shudder of his frame returned Grimka to his senses, he found he had descended the stair. Without awareness of his actions, he had passed silently to the lower landing. He crept across the chamber, leading with his hands to insure against bumping into furniture in the gloom. His breath came out in icy clouds; he saw motes of an exhaled plume swirl into the moonbeam from the window. His heart hammered through his chest—he could not fully account for the anxiety he felt.

As the roving clouds blackened the window, there came a loud creak at the top of the stair. Grimka saw in his mind's eye the precise board that had produced that groan under a stocky boot. He held his breath in the darkness, crouching between tables, as the thick soles clomped down the stairs.

There was a pause midway along the staircase. For a long moment, the phantom made no sound save a deep, malevolent seething that seemed to palpitate the very atmosphere — as though the hall itself were an organ contracting with each breath. Grimka felt a rhythmic pressure at his temples that threatened to make him ill. He lamented that his knife and hatchet were left by his bedside; in the dark, he slid his fingers along the tabletops, groping and praying silently for any sort of weapon.

"I know you're in there – you might as well come out–" came a husky, halting voice from the middle landing, where the stairs turned to overlook the room. Grimka went cold, for it was a voice belonging to no man he knew. Like the deer in the woods, he lay stiff in the shadows below.

Olynka's soft whisper hissed from the side parlor. "Where are you going? I can't go in there." There came a sharp intake of breath from the stairs, then a heft and grunt as the man on the stair vaulted his bulk over the banister and landed with a boom that shuddered board and beam. Grimka tensed in preparation, his lungs burning and his pulse banging painfully. His clammy hands seized on no weapon. The clouds shifted, and he saw the wood-cutter's axe shimmering as it passed against the silver-lit lattice. The black shape who wielded it was outlined before the parlor door.

The present threat to the girl (with the mystery of the second girl abruptly forgotten) stirred his limbs from their fear-induced torpor. He sprang at once. Right away, his shin banged against a three-footed stool which lay in shadow half-under the table by which he had crouched, and before it could topple entirely or rock itself aright, he had his hands on it and ran into the open, wielding it aggressively.

The dark stranger wheeled, raising the axe in defense. He managed only a partial turn before the stool clubbed him near the elbow, knocking the axe askew in his grip. Grimka followed with his entire bulk—which was not inconsiderable. He felt the superior weight of his opponent stagger and collapse as he wrapped his tight-corded arms about and drove on with his legs. Olynka screamed. The two men tripped over something in the blackness and went down together, overturning furniture with a tremendous din.

The widow was first to arrive, shouting and stumbling through the dark with her old crossbow in her arms; when Kasmir and Dieter arrived with arming swords, she let them pass. Yvorr came up last, holding his mace and a candle.

Only in the light did Grimka see that his hands were empty; the axeman had vanished from his arms, and he wrestled with nothing but a cushion and a tablecloth that had been dragged down in the tussle. The stool lay beside the door; one of its legs was dislodged and rolled slowly along. He scrambled about the floor, seeking his phantom attacker. Olynka was curled in the corner opposite the doorway, sheltering herself behind trembling hands.

“There was a man,” he cried, breathless. Frantic, he reached at the girl, grasping for her face. Her mother was there in a flash of white linen, instinctively separating them. Olynka clung to her shapely waist. Grimka felt Kasmir’s hand on his shoulder; not forceful, not restraining, but steady and steadying. “Did you see him?” he wailed. “Child, did you see the axe? Did you see the man with it?”

Her lip quivering, her cheeks shining in the candlelight, Olynka unburied her face from the folds of the widow’s dress and nodded.

CHAPTER 6

They all sat huddled round the largest table by the hearth in the great chamber, bundled against the midnight chill. The shutters were drawn, and the hearth dominated the room with its warm orange light—though the shadows always seemed to encroach upon it of late.

Olynka sat with them. The widow had at first been adamant on sending her back to bed, but she and Grimka had pleaded together until she relented. With gentle coaxing from Grimka, the girl described the fight from her perspective, starting with the hulking, shadowy man and his gleaming wood axe. To Grimka's great relief, her description matched his own memory of the terrifying and surreal incident.

When he prodded her, "Can you tell us about the other little girl I saw you speaking to?" The widow's wide eyes shot to her daughter's face. Olynka went silent under the scrutiny.

"Please, child," Grimka pressed. "You must be brave; it is too important."

Olynka clove only tighter to her mother, who sat rigid in her white blouse, gazing at him coldly. Slowly, Kasmir extended an open palm across the table. To everyone's surprise, the little girl placed her tiny white hand over his massive, calloused fingers. The widow tightened even further, as if to restrict her daughter, and glowered forbiddingly at the knight—all to no effect.

"Have no fear," Kasmir said into Olynka's bleary eyes. "I know that good Grimka shall believe your words, and so shall I."

Tremulous, she gazed into her mother's face, but the widow's chin was high, and her eyes had gone far away from the child. Gradually she began to speak, to the wonder of all:

"She is a good spirit. She is a little girl like me. She has always lived here, long before any of us came. Except perhaps for Mister Venslas…"

There came a creak at the top of the stair, and as one, the table turned, all on alert. Dieter even thrust back his chair, rising to face the interloper with his sword raised.

Old man Venslas stood there, gripping the rail shakily.

***

"I heard ye all afore," the venerable

bachelor said. His thick hose and long shirt hung from him in folds as though he had withered down within them; even his nightcap seemed to hang loose, revealing the shine of his scalp. Grimka and Kasmir eased him down the stair while Yvorr produced the plushest of the parlors' armchairs. Mladena poured him a drink and draped a shawl over his wizened shoulders.

"I know ye saw the little ghost girl down there. An' I know what stalks her."

When the widow began to protest, he cut her off: "Don't? Don't what? Upset the child? Disturb the dead? Open your eyes, woman! The child's upset an' the dead're awake!"

Had anyone other than Venslas spoken to the widow thus, no doubt he would be out on his ear. As it was, she looked shaken; then her chin ground forth while her whole jaw reddened, but at last, she lowered her eyes, at once forgiving and ceding. She buried her lips in her daughter's hair and breathed an apology into it.

"I was a boy when this very inn was built anew; I was at the raising of that barn—and the one afore it, that was torn down because it was built too close to the house. My father knew Agrym the innkeep who built her, and I knew their little girl—my own very age, she was. With all the building there was in the town, there was a great call for logging, and many a woodcutter came from the surrounding holds..."

Dieter let out a slow sigh; even Yvorr and Mladena seemed to merely bear through the old man's seemingly incoherent preamble. Grimka watched the knight, whose eyes were intent on Venslas' face. Kasmir had said his father was a sentry, and the huntsman felt a kinship for the sentry's son then, for in both professions, one never knew which information might prove crucial, and had to save it all in mind for later examination. Intermittently, the knight's eyes made their customary scribe's-pen motion, their focus far beyond the elder and the wooden beams beyond—perhaps they roved across the old barn and the lumber camps of yore. Grimka sensed with a surety those eyes saw many things clearly which were not apparent.

"... That winter, the snows came early and came deep. Three or four men were penned up in this inn more than a week. Buried in the blizzard with no way out. Them, and the innkeepers and their girl. One of them was this big lumber hand—don't have his name anymore—he was a tramp, come up from out of country looking for work. He could outhaul an ass, that tramp. Had shoulders like a melon cart and arms like oak. Small hands, though. I remember, even to me as a lad, those little hands looked queer on his big frame those times I saw him. Most of what anyone ever really found out about that night in the storm was what he told us—well, of course there was the *bodies*… and the *blood*—but there wasn't much he could tell as anyone could understand, for he was half out of his mind when he was found.

"From what could be found out, those men cooped up inside had only dice to pass the days. Dice and drinking. They diced and they drank and they cooked up a drunkenness between 'em—and anyone's been trapped inside in the snow'll tell you it does mischief to the mind. It was a poison pot they brewed between 'em, brewed of poison ingredients and nothing good. Folks supposed one soul or other was caught at cheating. Three or four men all drunk and bored and with rotten wits from sitting indoors, you could bet there was a fight over cheating, and bet it went ugly. That big tramp had handy his axe he used at the lumber yard, and he confessed to the killing. Killed one man over loaded dice, and when he saw what he'd done, knew he had to kill the rest. Had to kill em, or they'd tell. Killed one man, then the others. Chopped splitwise like he was used to doing logs. He confessed to it all. Chased down Agrym and his wife with no way out. Only the little girl gave him the slip."

Yvorr was surprised. "She got away? How?"

Sinking back into the musty plush chair, the elder mused. "Hmm. That's one question. The other is what happened to her? For nobody never found her. At least, *he* claimed not to. An'

I ten' to believe it." While he spoke, little Olynka fussed at her mother's hands, which were clapped ice-like over her ears. "They showed him the bodies, and he said it was all dim in his mind after a certain point, but he swore he never got the girl with his axe. The snow was piled high as that second window, and it was figured he crawled out that way to chase after her. We found him days after the snow, wandering around half-frozen and half-mad. His hands—queer, tiny hands on such a big man—were all black and ruined from frost. I saw them, myself, though they tried to keep me away. His hands went to gangrene; a few fingers fell off in the storm, and what're left were black, frozen around the handle of that bloody wood axe. He was all but barking when they found him; took a swing at someone just like he'd tried to do those poor others. The murder-madness gripped him almost nearly up to the end. They set him in a cell until he confessed, and then he was hung. Burned him on a pyre, as that's the only way he won't walk again. All but a finger or two he lost in the storm.

"The innkeeper's girl was never found. We figured she perished in the storm—poor thing—and wolves got up her remains. Back when the village was smaller, they were much closer, and after a storm like that early in the season, they'd get starving so bad they'd walk right into the middle of town after a bite. Take an old man right off his porch if they could. That's why she come back to haunt this place — it was her home. What you burn passes into the other realm. If you leave the bones unburnt…"

The sentence hung in the silence like an unfinished bridge. The wind picked up, and a blast of powder frosted the shuttered window. Air rushed down the flue and made the shadows cast by the great hearth dance. Grimka watched them, expecting the shades of the past to come leaping from them.

"That's why the inn went empty for some years. The innkeeper had one grown son, I recall. He went to the city and sold her off to the council. Said they might as well tear her down, but she's a strong house, a good old house. No one had the itch to go tear her down, and I've been glad for that, I have. So they nailed boards to her until Mladena and her husband come to buy her up. And she was strong as ever."

As the story went on, his speech slowed. His chest moved up and down slowly, accompanied by a low, tortured whistling. He yawned periodically, and his eyelids would droop every few moments until he caught them and corrected. Grimka drew his attention to the miniature sword above the door.

"We found that sword-symbol on the floor the other day; it had fallen from the hooks."

"Hmm." Said Venslas, as if in a dream.

"Can you tell us where it came from?" Grimka asked.

"Ah, yes. It came from a peddler up from the south. The innkeeper hung it up… was it your husband, dear? No? No, it was the old innkeep hung it up. That peddler said the old gods of the south are better magic against bad spirits, and Agrym was sore afraid of bad spirits. Ironic, if you think about it. Course, when the place changed hands it had to stay; it's bad luck to take down a token from your door, just like renaming a ship…" His head sagged, and he began to trail off.

"It's made of lead," said Grimka. "It's a cheap fake."

Venslas seemed to apprehend this gradually until he snorted. "Bah. Well, in't that the dambdest… no wonder it never scared the little girl off. Aye, I always knew it was her dwelt in this place; she never left. As for the other bloke, he must have just enough of himself left here… a hair, a shoeprint, a flake of skin off'n his nose… that he could sleep in this place until that spooky tramp came that night to wake him up. And once he woke up, all he could remember was that little girl who saw him commit his crimes and the unfinished business of shutting her up for good. He's looking for her, even at this minnit he's a-looking for her. And bad luck to be a little girl like our Olynka, a little girl herself. A shade has dim vision; one little girl might look the same as the next. And once he thinks he's finished that business, why then I reckon he's apt to take notice of all the rest of us, see that we've borne the same witness as she had to die for…"

He looked suddenly apologetic toward the widow and the child in her arms, as though by uttering these things, he had somehow caused them. Olynka valiantly fought sleep herself, though she appeared to be losing the fight – perhaps that was merciful. Another powdery drift gusted over the rattling window. Suddenly, Kasmir stood.

"Is there a priest in the village? A mystic?"

"Medicine woman, other edge of town," answered Yvorr, rising himself as if by instinct.

"How far?"

"Two. Maybe three miles."

"Take me," Kasmir commanded. "Let us not lose a moment."

"The sky bodes ill for travel," Grimka warned. "If the snow comes in earnest, it'll turn you out."

"All the more urgent it is, then. I fear the danger here is real and pressing. But if we act quickly enough, the falling stroke may be turned aside." Saying this, the knight nodded again to Yvorr.

Obediently, Yvorr followed him to the door, wrapping himself in the furs at hand without bothering to go upstairs for warmer undergarments.

"What am I to do?" asked Dieter. Going after them as they bundled themselves, he reached for his own cloak.

"I have known you all my life, cousin," the knight replied. "And you are nothing if not a man of strength. Be a comfort to these people, in your own way, until I return with what we need."

Turning to Grimka, he said quickly, "You are a hunter. Your trade is made by seeking that which eludes. The bones of the girl are buried on these grounds, I am sure. If your soul pities the soul of that innocent, then hunt, oh hunter, while the sentry stands over, and the emissary retrieves what is needed."

The brass latch clattered back and forth against the jamb of the wind-battered door, its tarnished surface rimed by the cold seeping from beyond. Kasmir lingered no longer than had the cat with the rat in its mouth, yet this was no nervous housecat but a lion flying with urgency of purpose. As he turned the latch, the door flew inward of its own power, driven by the weight of the wind and ice. An instant later, he and Yvorr were shadows in the swirling night; in another instant, they vanished into the black-and-silver chaos against the gloomy skyline of the shadowed barn. Grimka and Dieter were at the doorway, scooping aside little piles of building snow and pressing the door shut against the weight. When the icy howl was muted behind the oaken portal, Venslas' snoring became audible from his cushioned seat beside the susurrant hearth. The widow, returning from the kitchen where she'd left Olynka lying, went to his arm and shook him lightly, thinking to move him to his bed, but he slept deeply. Grimka bade her to leave him. It was a comfort to have everyone together on the ground floor.

CHAPTER 7

Grimka sat across the table from the old man. He gazed over the armchair's thread-worn back into the fire, trying to think. His thoughts were fuzzy with sleeplessness and strayed often. He felt the scrapes and bruises from the tumble with the night haunt: his elbow ached where it had struck either the doorjamb or a table; his knee had been scraped through his trousers on the floor; and a stiff and swollen feeling in his knuckles worried him. How many seasons of pulling a bow did he have left? Most often, he caught himself contemplating only the fire itself. His people had always held that fire is the gateway into the land of Paradise. Anything consumed by flame passed into the beyond and could not be sent back. Grimka tried to picture the heaps of firewood sitting around in the afterworld. Where did those logs go when burned again by the immortal shades of his ancestors? Only an old man, delirious, or an impetuous child could ever entertain such irreverent musings, he thought. Dieter slid another log into the fire and plopped into a seat at a remote table with a fresh toddy. He leaned the chair back on two legs with his feet crossed on the tabletop, holding the steaming cup in his lap.

The whole house seemed to sway on its beams under a particular blast of wind. The rafters creaked strenuously. The storm was becoming a blizzard in truth.

"Your liege might have been less eager," Grimka remarked. "I fear for him and my friend in this weather."

Dieter smiled. "He brooks no delay when his action has been decided. I cannot dissuade him from anything."

"Many a knight in legend took wisdom from his squire."

"Oh, Sir Kasmir has wisdom for the both of us," he said dryly. "His father pressed him into a yearning for philosophy. 'It is good to wield the sword – but only if one knows why.'"

"Why do you wield it?"

Dieter shrugged. Restrained irritation began to subtly drape his mien like a familiar cloak. "Maybe it's enough reason to be commanded to wield it. My liege bids me visit with the yokels. 'Be a comfort in your own way.' Here I am."

"And you do your duty fabulously, at that."

Dieter arched one eyebrow dangerously at the dry jape. Cocking back his nose and chin an inch, he studied Grimka, sitting slouched in his wooden chair, his thin nightclothes draped in the wolfskin, which seemed oversized without the layers of jerkin and coat. The squire chortled then, his snide aloofness forgotten in an instant of lost care. Grimka smiled too, and for a moment, they laughed together, low, self-conscious in the oppressive air of the haunted house. Dieter took his feet, hoisted his chair to Grimka's side, and set his toddy on the table between them.

"No doubt he is a singular man, Sir Kasmir – and his orders are singularly strange. What shall you do if our shade returns? Will he shrink when smitten with your sword?"

Dieter considered the arming sword, resting upright against a corner near the hearth. "I have seen shades and such things before," he said at length. "Some spirits deal in images as seriously as you and I deal in real things, and an object itself may be as important as what it represents. And as the cults of the South say, there is power in iron. I expect that any wight who wields an axe should respect a steel edge."

Though much of this remained wondrous, Grimka tried to take satisfaction in the squire's apparent confidence. "Hunting in the wild, there are signs I may follow to corner my quarry, yet a shade leaves no trace, like a wolf or boar, but seems to vanish here and appear there as it pleases, with no lair to track it to."

The wind rattled the casings. The black cat slunk into the room, yowling low at the walls, yearning to be among the tiny, frightened feet he heard scrabbling behind the planks. Old Venslas stirred over and moaned as though harrowed by some evil in his dream.

"Would that our little girl might appear and be so helpful as to point us to her bones," Dieter said dryly. The cat let out a hiss and edged toward the small parlor with a restive gnarr in his throat. "I pray you shall not need a shovel… or a raincoat."

All of a sudden, Grimka slapped his palm upon the table, giving the squire and the cat a start. Thrusting the chair away with a squeak, he leapt to his feet. "I've got it!" He cried. His eyes were on the parlor door. "The girl—the girl! She was leading Olynka on. What was it she said..? *'I cannot go in there'*! Do you see, Dieter, she was about to show the widow's daughter where to hide from the murderer!"

This speech was punctuated by

a thump from behind. The black cat gave a shrieking yowl and bolted to the wall nearby. He pressed against the loose panel and vanished into the sliver of blackness. Venslas turned over yet again; the widow stuck her head out of the kitchen; Dieter and Grimka turned to the door and beheld the leaden swordlet resting once more on the floorboards, with the blunted tip of its crescent blade pointed toward the parlor door.

CHAPTER 8

The two riders pressed through the blinding storm. The rising sun could not drive out the night. The squall became a gale and then a tempest. Soon, the horses could not bear them, and anyway, each gust threatened to tear a man from the saddle or topple him together with his steed, so they dismounted and led the miserable animals through cascading drifts of powder. Their garments, too thin to begin with, were no comfort against the stinging ice. Yvorr feared he would catch a chill, or worse. He slacked his pace so he could shout hoarsely into

Kasmir's ear:

"We will be lost in this blizzard. Whatever you need from the priest, can it not wait until the sky is clear?"

Kasmir hesitated—he knew his guide was right but was loath to reverse his chosen course.

"Three miles is far too far," he conceded. "Is there a smithy closer by? Or a potter?" His plan was incomplete, being mended on the fly, yet some premonitory instinct urged him to return with something, however desperate or inadequate.

"Farmer Godaman has a forge," Yvorr agreed. "We passed his drive not long ago. I saw the signpost."

"Does this Godaman own a crucible, Yvorr?"

"A what?"

"Steel!" the knight cried, his voice all but ripped from his lips by the furious elements. “Does he forge steel?”

“I don’t know. Maybe.”

“It’s chance enough. Take me there!”

***

The crawlspace behind the parlor wall was just wide enough for a child to move about with some freedom; Grimka, lacking the belly that tended to grace men his age before winter, could just manage to stand upright and sidle in the cobwebby gloom. Following the path of the arcing blade, he and Dieter had come to a section of wiggly wall paneling, much like the one in the hall. They scrambled for tools to widen the hole, inching the nails gently out. When the crawlspace was revealed, they discussed their next move. Dieter was too large to have any hope of maneuvering in there, but Grimka was just slight enough to manage—barely. The prospect of sending Olynka was floated and roundly dismissed.

There was no man alive who could impugn Grimka's steel or accuse him of any form of squeamishness. But these confines made him feel like a grape in a press. The intensifying storm filled his ears with its constant wail, unsettling the planks that hemmed him in. Every unsavory thing that man's unspoken heart knows to dwell in the lightless cracks under the earth crawled and slithered over his frame in a myriad of loathsome dreams. The tiny candle he held was more hindrance than help most of the time, its miserly glare clouded by dirty webs which he had to brush aside, taking strenuous care not to ignite anything – including himself. It was slow, nervous work.

His aches grew worse as he shuffled by slow inches through the confines – in particular, the inflammation around his knuckles. His arm and shoulder burned from the persistent task of holding the candle steady – switching it to the other hand was not an option. When the candle threatened to burn down to his fist, he replaced it from his pocket, lit the new one on the old, and snuffed the old one on his tongue – a trick he was glad to have learned in this limiting space.

He devoted the greater share of his concentration to steadying his breathing and the race of his heart. He tried not to imagine himself getting stuck, irretrievable, helpless until Dieter located him behind the wall and devised a way to rescue him. In other fantasies, he became so frenzied by the lack of air that he struggled until, in explosive madness, he burst the wall and came tumbling and scrambling out.

One worry that became particularly pervasive and vexsome was that his bladder would choose this time to nag him: a worry that seemed tenuously self-fulfilling. More than one rat scurried furtively from his feet, shuffling through inches of filth and dust. One time, something dropped onto the nape of his neck—something cold yet madly alive; he felt the roach's expanding pinions beat uselessly at his skin until it was righted, and then he heard the panicked clatter of its spiny legs through vibrations right into his skull. By sheer reflex, he sought to reach up with his back hand and swat the pest away but succeeded only in wrenching a muscle and scoring his elbow against a nail.

His breathing quickened; stale, frigid air rent through his sinuses and throat; his head spun, and the walls seemed to tighten against his chest and back. The roach buried its hot fangs into his neck, right over the bone. Thus vindicated, it scampered across his collar, tumbled disgracefully to the fathoms, and was gone.

He barely restrained himself from raising a foot to stomp on it and from crying shamelessly for help. The hunter fathomed, for the first time in his long life, how swiftly the mind can fly when the body is trapped. Old dreams, black dreams, unremembered, spread their pestilential wings across his vision. *How close are we all to madness,* a wild, arch voice hissed in his brain; *might a foot in a snare suffice to drive the precious white bird of reason to flight? – and then where does he roost? And will he roost here more?* This and other questions swirled through his mind in a toxic slurry. How long could one remain trapped and panicked? Would the mind snap, or the heart explode, in a merciful flash? He had to remain still for many minutes and collect himself, lest the feeling of literal helplessness overwhelm his wits.

Dieter thumped the wall some paces behind and yelled something indecipherable. Assuming what he could, Grimka shouted that all was well. In truth, he was desperate. It felt as though he had gone miles over hours, yet he knew it had only been inches, and by the rate he'd spent his candles, the hours numbered less than two. He longed to back out, even imagined how he could save face by claiming it was impassable, but he knew he could not do that.

His forward knuckle brushed a corner. Away from the main structure, there was a sloping recess into which he could not see. He inched forth, peering round the candle's dazzle. A beam crossed the crawlspace at the height of his shins, and he had to hunch under the second-story floorboards to squeeze over it. A tick or spider scrambled across his knuckles, and the flame wavered as he crushed it absently against the wall. He tore the webs away with his wrist and forearm. By tedious inches, the alcove came into view: a section of a forgotten cellar, little deeper than a sepulchral niche. He knew at once it had belonged to the old barn Venslas had spoken of, which had once abutted the house. Grimka thrust the candle in, his blood crashing like surf in his temples and ears. A shape slouched against the far earthen wall.

CHAPTER 9

There is a land of chaos and shadow, which lies between the world men see and myriad lands from which no mortal sojourner returns. In this shaded country, which is neither life and light nor death and darkness, images are matter, and belief lends strength to the believed. One who dwells here is as a man who dozes in the lower chamber while noisy lodgers cavort overhead; he cannot rest because they speak loudly; he is tormented by sleeplessness. This is why those who bury their kings do so in deep tombs under the cold earth, far from the influence of the living, who pierce the air with gaiety and with ire, and who, with their heedless touch, corrupt and alter the constant relics which the spirit remembers. Brooding in this spiritual limen was a beast of blackness that once was a man. Just as he was neither awake nor reposed, neither was he aware nor unaware of the men around the table as they gave voice to his plight and misdeeds. He drank of their worry — their belief in him and his power—and the worry of the mother and daughter — the way a plant is stimulated by the drops that feed it. A bloody instant, warped like a drumskin across eternity, mired his mind—an instant of rage and of gainless triumph — an instant of guilt, eternally witnessed.

The image of the child loomed, all-occluding in a brain disembodied yet embodied in will. That the guilt had been exposed and the sentence enacted was immaterial – for those had occurred in time, and this alien country lies outside of time. The crime and threat of exposure were the occupations in which he lived eternally. She had seen him, and she would tell. But in the country of twilight, there was yet time to silence his condemneress – time that would never stop running out. He hunted her over hours that were eons, scouring the narrow halls of the little house again and again and all at once. The girl was in this twilight land with him, and she was dwelling in the house beyond the brilliant threshold. The two were separate. The two were the same – in a land where form was substance, the further he believed it, the further it became so.

The suppositions, the frettings, the arguments, were offerings from the living, sacrifices on platters. The roots of the plant soaked up words. Their dreams gave form to his will. The seedling sprang into an oak. Swollen with new and sudden power, he stepped forth into the threshold of light.

***

Out in the hall, Venslas wrenched in his chair, gripped by wild and terrible visions. Dieter stood in the room beyond; he was intent on the travails of Grimka and dismissed the old man's groanings with no more than a glance across his shoulder. He did not notice when old Venslas rose from his chair as easily as a man one-third his age. The old man staggered a pace, then, seeming to find his stride, departed from the room. He was like a man in search of something lost. His eyes popped wide, but by looking into them, you could not say what, if anything, they landed on.

Just beyond the rear door, there was a tiny lean-to where the firewood was stored. Old man Venslas grasped the latch and thrust the door open. When the door opened, the moaning wind pitched into a scream. An icy gust shrieked up and down the flue, and the fire in the great hearth sputtered once and departed.

***

Grimka knelt into the tiny cellar. Crumbling earth walls, pierced by jagged roots, supported a roof of stone foundation. The child's mummified bones were gray, swollen with moisture, and brittle from fluctuating cold. She lay hunched, her sorry garments rotted away. She was doubled over, her hands near her neck as if in fervent prayer. As his numb hand brushed away the curtains of silver cobweb that clung to her, Grimka felt an overwhelming pity. He choked just as a shooting pain lanced through his aching knuckles.

She must have been trapped here,

he surmised. Even while her hunter, confused, drunk, and mad, went stumbling through the snow on a fool's chase, her foot got caught in the boards and stones, and the poor creature wasted away inside her own secret tomb.

Yet an investigation of her feet found them unobstructed. He could find no hindrance that may explain her entrapment. Had fear kept her paralyzed until the tragic end? Surely the freezing cold would have driven her out long before?

Grimka looked to the hands and raised his own fingers to his throat, imitating her pose. A lump was growing and itching deep within his trachea. He winced as another throb arced through his knuckles. The pain began to concentrate in the first joint of his longest finger. It felt as though someone was trying to tell him something.

Holding the candle out with his right hand, he balanced on his haunches and swept the earth with his left. He brushed aside wet and frosty clods, heaps of roach and spider husks, ages' worth of rat droppings until his fingers brushed something firm and smooth. He almost missed it, but he swept back until he found it again. It did not give when he squeezed it, and it was about the size of an almond shell. After fumbling the thing between nerveless fingers into the light, he recognized it: the first joint of a human finger.

His heart racing, he examined the girl's hands—the bones were complete. He let out a long, whistling breath as the truth of the girl's last terrible moments dawned upon him. Terrified, she had backed into the crawlspace. He gave chase and thrust a hand through the loose paneling to grasp at her.

Grimka remembered: when the murderer had been found wandering in the snow, his fingers had been destroyed by frostbite. His hands were small, delicate. With tremendous ferocity and luck, with the teeth placed just right, she could have severed the fingertip at the joint. He fell away, anguished; perhaps he faded from consciousness while she scrambled back into the remnant of the old cellar. Later, he went upstairs and escaped through the window.

And the knucklebone had lodged in her throat; he'd killed her, after all.

He stirred suddenly, intent on scooping the remains and bringing them up, before considering that he had no plan. With a ginger hand, he reached out but froze with a start.

He was touched at the wrist by a hand, white and gentle as moonlight — and as cold. When he gazed into the eyes of the little girl, the urgency on her face was plain.

"No," The shade breathed without breath. "Olynka!"

This was all that was spoken before a terrible gust swept the hall. The timbers rocked and bowed until he feared they would cave; with a howl like a great flute, the hearth in the hall was snuffed, and the star-like points in the wall cracks winked out at once. Then the wind, shrieking like a geist, swept around the corners in the crawlspace. It eddied in the alcove, throwing dust and refuse in a funnel. Grimka's candle went out in an instant and was torn from his grip. The spirit of the girl vanished along with the grisly surroundings. Then the wind flew up along the crawlspace like a chimney after some distant channel to the frost night air; Grimka was alone, and all he could hear was Dieter shouting in the great chamber.

CHAPTER 10

Dieter wheeled as soon as the hall was plunged into darkness, his fingers flexing and reaching instinctively for steel. The breeze toppled candles, snuffing most, and set the suspended oil lamps rocking crazily on their chains. Deep shadows churned along each surface. The wind whistled in his ears with a chill which stung his skin and seemed to go deeper than flesh. In the scintillating gloom, he spied the beshadowed form of the old man and the inconstant glint of the dull iron wood axe. He ran for his arming sword in the corner near the hearth.

Venslas tromped toward the kitchen. Dieter rushed to bar his way.

"Ghast!" He bellowed, stepping in front with his sword upraised. "Step out of that old man, or see me carve you out!"

The thing possessing the body of Venslas squared up. The bent spine straightened into a posture that was not his. The axe was ready to meet the blow of the sword. Through black, rolling eyes, it sneered at him, a sneer no soul had ever imagined on the face of Venslas.

The widow was at the doorway with her crossbow raised, but when the lamplight danced over his face, she threw it down with a cry: "Venslas!" To Dieter, she said, "You can't!" Repeating this, she flung her arms around his elbow, vainly trying to pull him back. Dieter cursed, rebuffing her easily; she rose again in a frenzy and clamor to end the fight. She must have supposed they had quarreled or that Dieter, whom she little trusted, had taken to robbing. They were tangled once more, and Dieter's head was turned toward her—almost fatally.

The axe swung with surprising speed—for it was not the arms of the elder but the will of the ghost that drove it. The widow had his swordarm more forcefully this time, and he struggled to drive her off without harming her badly. He caught sight of the thick iron blade and dove to the floor just before it would have entered his brain. He and the woman fell prostrate. Olynka was at the kitchen door, and she let out a scream. The ghoul turned from the two wrestling forms at his feet and stalked toward her.

Dieter cursed again and scrambled to his feet, disentangling himself, this time with little fear of harming the widow, with whom he was truly annoyed. His ire was rising, and he slapped and kicked her away while she clung to him, seeking to drag him down.

"Damn you, girl, run! Damn you if you don't run!" He left Mladena floundering as he took his feet. His sword was up, ready to run the old man through from the back. But a snatch at his trouser cuff stayed him again. Kicking her off once more, he rebuked her: "He's mad, don't you see? He means to slay your daughter. Now stay off!" Olynka screamed again; again, Dieter swore. The old man's spine presented itself through his thin night frock as he readied a strike. Mladena felt along the floor until her hand rested on the crossbow. The bolt was still in place; she wheeled onto her back in the spinning shadows. Sitting upright as best she could, determined to rescue her friend and tenant, she peered down the shaft at the form of Dieter as he leveled his point.

***

Grimka scrambled hands first, groping along the tight corridor. His heart pounded painfully, and he choked on fetid dust. Edges of nails and rough boards scraped him at every move. He slapped his hand against the interior wall. He had no sense of distance in the utter dark and dreaded that he would pass the opening. He overheard enough to surmise, at least in part, the terrible events in the great hall. He did not know if he could free himself in time – or even what he could do if there was time.

CHAPTER 11

The wight's spine writhed aside as the steel tip sliced in; rather than impaling and severing the vital nerve, the sword split wide the wispy nightgown and drew a streak along his ribs. The bolt from the crossbow whipped past Dieter's head, shattering a glass bottle high beyond the bar. He shot back a scathing look, even as Venslas turned his attention from the girl onto him. In the moment of distraction, the girl found her boldness and sprinted. She made for the open side door but hesitated at the sight of the elements bowling through. Single-minded, seeming not to feel its grievous wound, the hulk of Venslas lumbered on while Dieter dogged him apace. He brandished out his red steel, glimmering dully in the wavering lamplight. Confronted, the mute creature balked. "You have felt the edge," Dieter taunted. "Now you know respect for steel, wight. Do you see your own blood among his? I see that you do. Know fear, and kneel."

The widow dashed across the boards to her daughter, tossed the bow aside, and scooped her up. Her hair in wild tangles caught the scintillations of the weakening lamp. Their faces were both as white as the dying flakes that cascaded about them. As the woman's arms sheltered the girl's body, the mother's face cast about, wondering where to go. Up the stair, to be cornered, or into the storm, to freeze? Helpless, she dragged herself and her clinging daughter into a beshadowed corner where they sobbed, fearing and despairing—for themselves, for each other, and for the goodly Venslas.

With a sudden motion, the ghast hammered his axe. Dieter knocked his blade under the head; bracing a hand over his sword arm he drove the blow aside, taken aback at the resistance he met. He made a swift grab for the handle while their weapons were binded, but the spirit of the murderer gave a canny shift that forced Dieter to retract his bare fingers. Instead, he pivoted with his opponent, stepping into the turn. Turning his blade across his chest so the axe slid wide of his body, he smashed his pommel into his opponent's face. Venslas reeled, as much from the graze as from the touch of steel, the mark of Man's warlike wisdom and will to dominate. Dieter pressed the attack, but the ghost had skill in arms, and again, the squire was astonished by the speed of the axe. The two squared off a pace apart. Dieter made sure to keep the women at his back.

***

Grimka scrambled through the hole in the wall, scraped and bleeding, into the hazy and fluctuating light. Through the doorway, he could see into the hall, saw the women curled about each other, and saw the flashing sword and axe. Beyond, the flapping door barked against the wall, straining on its hinges like a tethered hound and belching crystals that flashed as keenly as the squire's steel. The light swung over, and he saw the blood on Venslas' side and groaned. Lifting himself wearily, he rushed forward, shouting to Dieter, "Fool, what have you done? Are you blind, that you do not see the man cloaking the ghast? Have a care for your soul, lest you end up like him!"

Over the screeching gale, Dieter

screamed: "What would you do?"

Grimka's feet stopped in place, remembering that he had no answer to the question. If he could reach the women... He must get them out of the house. But then what? Might the spirit chase them as he had when he was yet a man? Mordek had been right; it should have been done long ago. How had they all failed to notice how dire things had become?

If he only had a weapon, he thought... Then he looked toward the entry, to the emblem resting in the doorway, and a desperate plan of heroism took form in his mind.

***

Two men and two horses pushed through the snow. The tempest torrented about them, negating the rising of the sun, keeping them in perpetual grayness. Yvorr trudged ahead, knee-deep sometimes and sometimes up to his waist, clearing the powder for the horses; Kasmir pushed the sledge from behind. Though they had taken new clothes from the smith and a wide shovel, the trek was slow and miserable.

Atop the sledge was their principal purchase. Godaman had been quizzical, to say the least, to find Yvorr knocking in this weather, all the more when the knight's request was relayed. Kasmir would explain neither his reason for obtaining a crucible nor the urgency with which it was needed. It was possible he hardly knew himself and was grasping at a second-rate, half-formed plan, acting more on intuition than insight. Or perhaps his apprehension was of a superstitious nature – as though the forces of the spirit world might hearken to his plan and undertake to thwart it. The crucible was only fit to hold a gallon.

Kasmir had lamented that a larger one could not be obtained, but Yvorr was grateful, for the thick clay vessel was a practically unbearable burden in these conditions. Godaman and his sons attested that it took two men to lift it into the furnace and three to remove it when it was cool and full of steel. Kasmir paid for it by trading his own sword.

They had switched positions many times, and Yvorr began to fear they were lost. Just then, the gray hump of the barn loomed out of the storm at their side. Several paces further, and they arrived at the front of the inn. Wind-blown snow piled the facade all the way to the second story window. The window peeked down, dimly lit and barely visible, like a perching gargoyle at the top of the great drift, as it must have done on a dark day long ago.

"It will take hours to dig to the

door!" Kasmir's hoarse bellow cut the shrieking wind.

"The side door is in the lee," Yvorr answered, moving to be heard. "Might be it isn't covered yet."

Kasmir nodded, brushed his gloves against his coat, and took the handles of the sleigh. They were nearing the corner when a scream reached their ears as if whistling through the seams of the house itself.

The two men pulled up, looking at each other. "That was not the wind," Kasmir said.

"Mladena," Yvorr agreed.

Kasmir rushed past, abandoning the sledge and pushing through the tireless snow. In an instant, he was beyond the cornerpost, swallowed up by swirling ice. Yvorr rushed to unharness the horses and slapped their rumps. They trotted off toward the barn. An instant later, he was at Kasmir's heels as the snow lapped up around the sledge and its cargo.

CHAPTER 12

Dieter had tried many times to get the old man disarmed. He cursed — had the dotard hunter not stirred his conscience, he would surely have done with this farce by now. But he had become afraid of further wounding the man — and he'd have to answer for the bruises on the widow, too.

The old man was growing more cunning. Observing that Dieter strove to keep the girls behind him, he angled his attacks in such a way to force Dieter into awkward defenses. He began to sense, too, that Dieter was reluctant to do him serious harm, and he exploited this by ramping up his aggression, leaving vital openings a less scrupulous opponent would surely take. The spirit did not tire, yet the soreness in Dieter's sword arm was progressing into numbness under the punishing work of parrying the swift and brutal blows. Absent some change, Dieter thought he would soon be forced to end it in his own way — and just let them all hate him for it. He cursed Grimka again.

Near the front parlor, Grimka gave a shout, and the women went scurrying to his side, taking refuge in the small room. Venslas made to pursue them, but Dieter headed him off. The squire allowed himself a sigh of relief. With a wall between them, he had more options for space, but would that be good enough?

Grimka was there, brandishing the

leaden sword totem. Invoking the god he had learned of from Kasmir, he cried, "I abjure you by Dek's power!"

The ghast regarded him coolly. Dieter stepped in, but Venslas warned him off with a warding strike.

"You do not know how to use that," the ghast grumbled.

"I know how to use it," Grimka said. His trembling hand lifted the sign higher. His arthritic knuckles bulged and whitened sorely about the handle. He set his jaw, returning the ghost's glare as boldly as he could with watering eyes. "The god from the South himself dwells within, shade, and you will not resist his will."

The ghost sneered, yet stepped back. The axe remained at the ready. Dieter watched, seizing the reprieve. He studied Grimka carefully, his face plain with doubts.

The ghast glanced to the squire, bolstered by what he seemed to see there. He stayed immobile, at bay. Grimka flushed. The change in the ghoul's face alarmed him, and he feared losing this battle of spirits. Yet he sensed too a genuine power in the emblem he held, counterfeited though it was. He wished to believe the shade would feel it, too, if he asserted it strongly enough. He commanded his shaking foot to inch forth.

"Dek has defended this house, and you shall —" The axe swung.

Grimka let out a piteous cry. The lead symbol clattered to the boards, cloven raggedly and nearly bisected. It landed among a smattering of blood and bouncing bits of flesh.

Blindly, Grimka fell, clutching at the spouting stumps of his knuckles. He groaned and writhed and wrapped the nubs into his breast. The linen bloomed blackly with blood. Frenzied at the sight, Dieter leapt onward with his blood-flecked sword. Again and again, the weapons clashed. The axehandle held many notches; chips of wood and flakes of congealing blood mingled in the crystalline flurry that streamed from the open door. Dieter seized on a new idea: if he could strike the handle in the same place enough times, he might disable the axe enough to get close for a takedown. What he would do next, he had no time to consider. If only Kasmir had not gone away.

As if in answer to the prayer, a black shape was at the door. As it flew across the chamber, Dieter recognized his mighty master. "Dieter, the axe!" he cried, even as he rushed in. Old Venslas wheeled at the shout, striking downward. Kasmir rolled his shoulder and leaned in. The shaft landed above his left breast, and the two collided. Though Kasmir was the far larger man, they wrestled on their feet. The knight worked to bind the old man's arms. He managed to pin the axe high, long enough for Dieter to reach it. The squire threw his sword aside – it landed atop its leaden double – and with both hands gripping the long handle, he disarmed Venslas. Yvorr was at their side. He kicked the axe away after Dieter threw it down and helped the squire and knight drag Venslas to the floor.

Picking himself up, Grimka felt the widow press into his side, Olynka still trailing at her skirts. "Grimka, poor Grimka!" she cried.

"This?" Grimka gave a poor, pale smile. "No, darling, fear not for me." He pressed her close, and she clove to his breast and wept. He felt his heart swell with pity for her and for the child. He embraced her, keeping his maimed hand tied in his shirt, and on impulse, kissed the top of her head. The widow's dusty hair smelled of sweat, yet he thrilled with the detectable essence of *her.* Sorely, he imagined all the things he longed for the power to do in her service.

The ghast bucked, mad with outrage, yet his unnatural might could not shirk the great weight of Sir Kasmir and his two accomplices. Holding his shoulders to the floor, Kasmir spoke in a calm voice.

"Hear me," he said. "Remember. Your crimes are past; your trial was given, your sentence carried out. You must remember what you have forgotten, and do not add to the sins that brought you to this state."

Venslas was weeping with gritted teeth. Bearishly, he growled, uttering confused lamentations and protestations.

Kasmir shook him firmly but not viciously. The old man's frame was under his power, but he spoke to the alien soul within. "Remember! You were caught. You were executed. Your crime was repaid—do not compound it! Return Venslas his body, and go forever from this place."

A change came over Venslas then. His struggling diminished and then ceased. The snarling visage gave way to a perplexed expression, then ceded to one of dawning clarity. Yet the possessor still held possession; it was the Mien of the spirit that had changed.

"I am trapped," Venslas croaked, barely audible. Grimka pressed away from the widow. Kneeling in the mess, he scoured the floor. Scattered among his own lost fingers, he found the one belonging to the murderer.

"The funeral was incomplete," he

declared, presenting the old knucklebone to the room. "I found this behind the wall—with the remains of a child."

The shade's face lit with profound recognition, and his eyes were fully astream. Kasmir said, "Well done —" then, turning back to Venslas, he said, "We have the means to burn you rightfully if you will turn from your anger and accept our mercy."

The shade tried to buck him. Again, it struggled, in vain. "I accept," he uttered at last and departed.

CHAPTER 13

Over the following hours, a gradual calm settled over the inn. Venslas fell into a slumber, barely breathing. They pulled the narrow bed from the kitchen and laid him on it in the great hall, the better for the widow to keep an eye on both him and Grimka. Impatiently, the latter let his wound be looked at, while urging her to see to Venslas. He had experience dressing his own wounds—though none as serious as a hand with missing fingers. Yvorr helped him gather the pieces of his ruined hand, picking them up delicately like shards of pottery and placing them in a bowl. "Long have I feared my days of archery were near an end; finally, I put my worries to rest," Grimka joked, and Yvorr chuckled despite himself. They all were tired but knew much work was yet to be done. The air was lighter but remained cold. Kasmir had permitted the stove to be rekindled but insisted the great hearth stay unlit.

As soon as the wind was low, he and Dieter went out into the snow to uncover the crucible. The clouds were parting, and already the sun was hardening the frost into ice. Together, the three men lifted the crucible into the hearth and filled it with coals from the last fire. Kasmir took a mortar and pestle from the kitchen and ground the murderer's knucklebone so that it would burn. Before the crucible was lidded, as an afterthought, the widow added in the ruined leaden swordlet. "It is time to bring a new god into this hall," she explained. When a large fire was lit, the copper shutters on the hearth's sides were closed, and Dieter worked the bellows with vigor. The hearth became a furnace. The heart of the inn pulsed with an overbearing heat, and thick, black smoke shot out from the chimney.

It was agreed without discourse that the girl's remains must be exhumed and burned as well. Helpful ghost though she might be, a proper rest was hers by right. Grimka led them to the wall, his best estimation of where he'd found her. Reverently, they pried the panels and pulled her out in pieces. She would be taken to the priest when the weather was better. They laid her on a table with care and draped her in a curtain. Grimka sobbed to see her so respectfully arranged. "I wish it were spring, so she might have flowers to hold," said Olynka, tearfully. Yvorr found some long sprigs of dry rosemary and thyme, and together, he and Olynka wove garlands.

After each task, the atmosphere seemed lighter.

Kasmir and Dieter lingered a few more days. Venslas never awoke; the sledge bore him to the priest along with the old bones of the young girl. The crucible was slow in cooling. After it was removed, it cracked open to reveal a single cake of brittle carbon slag. This, too, was given over to the temple. Dieter apologized earnestly for the loss of the old man – and for the bruises to the widow—but none of the inn-dwellers could impeach him with confidence; they all admitted his part may have stemmed disaster, and no one was sure they could have done anything better. Kasmir refused any payment for the exorcism—though he accepted the return of his arming sword at a fair price – he only bade them all remember his friendship. They vowed they always would.

Confiding later in Kasmir, Dieter said, "Shall the old man's death mark my soul? I now see what else I could have done – so many other things – yet I reached only for the sword. Only when it's too late do I see the other ways." Kasmir listened to him, and for a long time, he said nothing.

Then he said, "I think my soul is as marked as yours." When Dieter scoffed, he insisted: "In truth, I believe it. Where was I? I set off from the start with a very poor plan; a plan which became worse when I doubted and changed course. It came to resemble nothing I had intended, and it made no difference. Truly, in the end, I cannot see what difference I made that I could not have made by staying."

The vagabond necromancer was never again seen. Word came over the spring melt that a similar man had been hanged by some villagers many miles East. Nobody ever confirmed that it was the same man who had summoned the ghost in the inn. Nobody ever found out if he was a Riav. With his hunts (and, therefore, his travels) behind him, Grimka paid far less attention to rumors abroad. But when the Village Council announced they would bend the knee to the new king, Cideffrid, he found he was glad.

The villagers came to revere him by the moniker of "Old Knucklebone." The way some told it, the name came because he'd discovered the old knucklebone of the killer; others rather derided him, using the new name to remind him of the old knucklebones he'd lost. Old Knucklebone himself would answer by boasting with a wink that he'd invented a sure-fire cure for arthritis — though his *other* hand still pained him.

The space above the doorway was adorned at last with the traditional idol of the Tribefather and his hospitable spirits – a totem welcoming all and any goodly souls. Though Grimka could do little work and had little saved to pay his board, the widow took him in for good. He helped in the ways he could, even aging and one-handed. To the ladies of the inn, he became, each in various ways, a peculiar mix of brother, father, and husband. He saw Olynka recover her vitality over seasons, bloom into womanhood, find a husband, and go off to begin a new house. He outlived Yvorr, by chance, and in the old age of the inn, some boarders came and went, but it was largely just Grimka and Mladena. His love was kept kindled and close to his heart, yet distant from its object. In light of his glimpse of the afterlife, he bore ever in mind the eventual day when the two of them would be confronted by her husband within the eternal veil.

Against that day, and as a constant reminder, Grimka kept his own knucklebones tied in a satchel beside his breast. He touched them, whether devoutly or by impulse, throughout the day – just to reassure himself they had not been lost. For he was determined that they should go with him into the pyre.

END

P. J. Atwater lives with his wife and three children in Southern California, where he works as an education specialist. He holds a B. A. Degree in English Literature and spends his free time in his private library with works of history, philosophy, and classic literature.

Twitter/X: @PJ_Atwater
Instagram: @atwatertales
Facebook: P J Atwater Writing
Web: atwatertales.com

www.ingramcontent.com/pod-product-compliance
Lightning Source LLC
LaVergne TN
LVHW090611110826
845146LV00001B/343